THE LIVING STATUE

Günter Grass

THE LIVING STATUE
a legend

translated from the German
by Michael Hofmann

A NEW DIRECTIONS PAPERBOOK ORIGINAL

The Living Statue is published by arrangement with Steidl Verlag

Originally published in German in 2022 as *Figurenstehen: Eine Legende*
First published as New Directions Paperbook 1612 in 2024
Manufactured in the United States of America

Library of Congress Cataloging-in-Publication Data
Names: Grass, Günter, 1927–2015, author. |
Hofmann, Michael, 1957 August 25– translator.
Title: The living statue : a legend / Günter Grass ;
translated from the German by Michael Hofmann.
Other titles: Figurenstehen. English
Description: New York : New Directions Publishing Corporation, 2024.
Identifiers: LCCN 2024031968 | ISBN 9780811238106 (paperback) |
ISBN 9780811238090 (ebook)
Subjects: LCGFT: Novels.
Classification: LCC PT2613.R338 F5413 2024 | DDC 833/.914—dc23/eng/20240711
LC record available at https://lccn.loc.gov/2024031968

10 9 8 7 6 5 4 3 2 1

New Directions Books are published for James Laughlin
by New Directions Publishing Corporation
80 Eighth Avenue, New York 10011

THE LIVING STATUE

Nowadays the remains are museum pieces, hard as rock, but back when the Wall was still standing, as though by force of habit, and the powers either side of it continued to bark at each other, though at reduced volume, an invitation came fluttering onto my desk, which without much thought I accepted. The names of venerable towns—Magdeburg, Halle an der Saale, Jena and Erfurt—promised a journey back in time. I was told I would need to be patient, but the application had been filed. While we waited for leave to enter the exclusive workers' and peasants' state, I started browsing in my recollections of the Middle Ages, in varying company, over peppery meat dishes, various pickled parts, along with groats of buck-wheat and millet sweetened with honey. When after the customary delays—twice the application was turned down—the stamped papers arrived, the itinerary was fixed, leaving opportunity for—albeit brief—stops on the way, in Quedlinburg and Naumburg, places whose history was recorded in the textbooks of my school days.

Many a time I had fed historic guests. Once I sat with a hangman and some of his clientele over tripe, once shared a table with the commanders of Teutonic orders. Appropriate to Friday, I set a dish of fried Scanian herrings before Dorothea von Montau. Afterwards, Dorothea, a somewhat eccentric lady, recited some of her verses to us in Middle High German, betraying, so it seemed to us, some of the influence of the minnesinger Wizlaw von Rügen, and yet were all her own work. Scanian Herring was the title of the chapter in the novel.

Our first station was Magdeburg. A Lutheran pastor there by the name of Tschiche, whose sons had conscientiously objected to serving in the National People's Army, and were therefore obliged to provide alternative service in construction brigades, had shown similar doggedness and patience in his communications with lay and clerical authorities, and finally had prevailed: we were permitted to enter the German Democratic Republic, and I was slated to read in sundry churches and parish halls from my most recently published book, which dealt with rats and humans. I have always enjoyed reading aloud. If pressed, then also in sacred spaces with long-tested acoustic properties. The Middle Ages, I told myself, actually felt more remote to us than the Roman Empire. There were more discoveries to be made in the Eastern Harz, say, in Quedlinburg, than on the Via Appia. We slept in run-down parsonages, where a short grace was spoken before meals. Creaking floorboards. Musty foundations. Corpulent ministers' wives.

During our tour, the state espionage service showed commendable restraint, even when in Halle the overflowing parish hall was abruptly forsaken, and a nearby Catholic church with amplification spontaneously pressed into service. On page after page, it was recorded how the surviving rats practiced walking upright. Each time, I would read for over an hour, followed by questions. They came, hesitantly to begin with, then without inhibition from the audience cramming the pews and rows of wooden chairs: "Is it better to stay? Or apply to leave?"—I said: "The other side is only the other side." But that was something my questioners would one day find out for themselves.

The distance from one century to another was no more than a hand's breadth. In Erfurt, where Luther, then still a monk in Augustinian orders, had first learned to question, I read surrounded by the old walls. A group of GDR punks turned up with the aim of disrupting my reading, but were quickly seduced by my tale of rats, set at the time of the flagellants, when it was reported the Jews had villainously introduced the plague. The present-day state and its organs appeared almost exhausted. In Jena the minister and his wife and children kept a horse, which as in the fairy tale loomed over the stable door. Heretics were pursued, then as now; a succession of wars given names and dates. In Thuringia there were reports of Waldensian refugees from Bohemia. The crooked parsonage stood in a shabby hamlet not far from the battlefields of Jena and Auerstedt. I saw signposts to them. Wherever I looked, there was the crumble of Gothic. And the present too, however rigid its political control claimed to be, was turning into history at the edges.

Whom should I now ask to dine? Magdeburg, where I read in the cathedral refectory, came up with my first candidate: the lugubrious general Tilly, the commander of the Papist forces, fresh from torching and looting the city, invited himself. I set before him a sweet-and-sour dish of blood soup with chopped kidneys, called *Schwarzsauer*.

Then we availed ourselves of a day off between events. All around us were the battlefields of the Thirty Years War. Or was it not until after Erfurt, on the return leg, that we were tempted to divert? No, it wasn't Weimar that drew us, or Buchenwald, now presented as a memorial forever adjacent to it. Whither, then? No doubt, our journey had given us second sight: "Why don't we go to Naumburg, maybe they'll have the cathedral open?"

Some time in the late '80s. Late spring, possibly? No, it was fall. I see, or seem to see, heavily laden apple trees in the front gardens. In any case, when we saw the gray forms of Naumburg huddled around the cathedral, we saw smoke from the chimneys gradually dispersing. The town's alleyways reeked of brown coal. A smell more sour than bitter. No rain, the Saale was some way off. It was anyone's guess where its tributary the Unstrut ran. As in many towns in the workers' and peasants' state, the old buildings seemed to be falling apart in slow motion; to live here would be to chronicle decay. The slab constructions of our new age kept themselves to themselves some way off. We didn't see anything special. The cathedral was closed for lunch. In a square bordering a parklike space, there was an open sausage stand. My wife was in the mood for an East German bratwurst. Years earlier, when the Wall was built across Berlin, she had run away from her native state. She still talked about "Western money" when she was totting up D-marks, or was pleased with some economies she'd made while shopping. She hailed the Eastern sausage: "Tastes the same as ever." And I thought it appropriate to remark: "At least it doesn't smell of Wessi currywurst."

No one spoke to us. And we didn't speak to anyone. Our car, a Swedish model, stood legally parked somewhere. There wasn't a bench anywhere. We hoped not to draw attention. Time here passed differently. Blocked off to the front, it seemed to go in reverse. Ever since I was a boy, I'd wished I could be hidden away in a different period. Not the crampedness of our two-room apartment, nor the later life in camps and barracks, nor any noisy children of my own, could ever keep me from slipping away from the present time. Then, before long, I would find myself in a different society. On paper you could do anything.

When the cathedral opened after lunch, we were obliged to take an official guide. The first item on our agenda was the Romanesque crypt, then it was the turn of the Eastern choir, and then we had the architectural features of the late Romanesque nave pointed out to us, but all I can recall is the guide's windy and rather bossy account of the Western choir with the rood screen. A young woman in a Chairman Mao suit addressed herself to us and three other couples. Her somewhat pedantic German had the merest touch of a Thuringian accent. She preferred the plural form. "We see here a piece of early

Gothic architecture …" "After examining the relief either side of the entry to the rood screen, we now turn our attention to the figures of the twelve donors …" "Now we look at the most familiar couple …" We—a group only two of whose members were noticeably wearing Western garb—we followed her instructions.

As soon as I cast my mind back, we are stepping through the Western rood screen into the choir, instantly disappointed by the scale of what the guidebook claims are the life-sized figures of the donors. We had imagined them elevated on pedestals under carved stone canopies. That's how it is with originals. They only represent themselves. We had been duped by the familiar photographs showing us the supposedly monumental Konrad and Gepa, Hermann and the smiling Reglindis, the pensive Timo and the choleric Sizzo, Gerburg and Wilhelm, and most of all, the Margrave Ekkehard beside the quizzical Uta. As was remarked by one of the three couples that with us clustered around the guide: "Oh, but they're so much smaller than I expected …"

We had to come to terms with the size in which

they presented themselves, and also with the vestigial scraps of color that irregularly and distractingly adhered to their forms. Any attempt to envisage the donor figures in their original color was doomed to futility. So we did what we could to view each image in its current condition as an original. Our guide's expatiations made no reference to the faded color, nor to the misleading photographs, which made use of good lighting and carefully selected angles. The acoustics of the Western choir gave her every word its dogmatic significance: "These single or paired donor figures have been standing here exactly as we see them now since the year 1250. All except for the one called Konrad, who in 1532 in the course of a mysterious maliciously started fire—the choir stood in flames—fell from its plinth and was subsequently and a little inadequately rebuilt. We are in the presence of the work of an anonymous master of the early Gothic period, even though the realistic style of the folds does not accord with the mannered pleats of that time …"

She delivered her lines as convincingly as though she were saying them for the very first time. We were shepherded along the left side of the choir. A faint but distinct pedagogic compulsion was intended to prevent any straying, much less a lingering in front of the renowned, exemplary and oft-acclaimed couple. We stood in front of the uncrowned Gerburg and the one-time fallen Konrad. When we looked up to see Hermann and the coroneted Reglindis, I heard one of our couples whisper to each other: "Look at her smile, it's just like your sister Elvira, a little bit mocking."—"You're right, that's our Elvira, exactly."

Maybe the whispering didn't escape our leader and guide: "People say our donors have such a remarkably naturalistic expression that they seem to have been taken from life. Maybe so—even if this so-called naturalism is only an expression of our own subjectivity, and not a true criterion for a work of art. What is the case, though, is that each donor has been created as an individual. Hence their effect on us. We feel their resemblance to us, and yet they belonged to the ruling class, and as we'll see in a moment with Margrave Ekkehard II and Uta his wife, they are all too aware of the fact. They were the movers and shakers of their age. In the case of Ekkehard, he was a warrior, a land-grabber, and a terror to his inferiors, ruling the Slavic people east of the Saale with a heavy hand. He is even said to have murdered one of his fellow landowners. But great artists like our Naumburg master succeed, as we see here, if not in suspending class contradictions, at least in making them appear transparent."

Finally, we were standing before the couple of all couples. Our guide and leader gave the merest hint of a smile, as though indulging our impatience. She stands there where she has always stood, to the left of him, and keeps her face half-concealed behind the right raised part of her collar. And since her expression is one more or less of dismissal, one can see the raised collar as expressing some reserve to the man with her. Exactly, and there already were some whispers from our group: "Wouldn't you say she looks a bit mad at her old man ..."

The donor figures in the west choir of the Naumburg Cathedral have been subject to the most contradictory interpretations: secret romance, the expectation of salvation and, during the Nazi years, a lot of nationalist nonsense. Thus, of Reglindis, variously described as smiling, grinning or even sniggering, it was said that this Polish princess exhibited unmistakably Slavic features, and was grinning like a charwoman, whereas our true Nordic Uta … And so on. Even though we have little information about the origins and circumstances of the donor figures, there is no shortage of theories or claims. Reports persisted of a love affair between Uta and Wilhelm von Camburg, the husband of the historical Gerburg. But the only certain facts we have are that Uta came from an Ascanian noble family and her marriage with the margrave remained childless.

And so we duly heard: "We have little information about the social and economic background of the donors. It has been conjectured that the Naumburg master was acquainted with French cathedral architecture of the time, possibly including the sculpture at Rheims, so barbarously destroyed in the First World War. But let us not lose ourselves in speculation. Let us open our eyes and our minds to the beauty and expressiveness of these stone portraits."

We accordingly opened our eyes and our minds to

the sculptures, or prepared to do so. My wife, who all the while we were inspecting the donor figures, did not speak, is called Ute. She was born when the cult surrounding Uta of Naumburg and the Bamberg horseman was at its height; many girls born in the midthirties were christened Uta or Ute. Of course, while I stood in front of the woman with the raised collar, it didn't occur to me to compare Uta and Ute, comparisons, they rightly say, are odious, but just then, on our little side trip to Naumburg, I felt a little twinge.

I'll invite the lot of them, I said to myself so emphatically that it might have been a resolution. The invitations will go like this: "On the anniversary of my visit to Naumburg Cathedral, when the Wall was still standing …" But where should I send them? And whom should I ask? The historical originals, of whom apparently so little is known? The Margrave Ekkehard II, who in the eleventh century did battle with Sorbian and Polish armies, or some Ascanians or other? Or should I issue them to the persons who stood model to the Naumburg Master? Because in his workshop he will have worked from whichever cheery or miserable individuals from the vicinity he had at his disposal. The donors, whoever they were, merely supplied their names. But a leering type like Reglindis or the lump of sadness that became known as Timo, they were frequenters of Naumburg's pubs and back alleys. And what period? Towards the middle of the thirteenth century, two or three years before the confirmed date of 1250, when the Staufers' imperium was beginning to crumble, shortly before Frederick II lost his life in some Apulian miasma or from Papal poisoning. Just before the onset of the so-called Dark Ages. But what did they know in Naumburg of the events in distant Palermo? Did some sense of the coming of a new age move the Master of Naumburg and his models?

I invited all twelve of them to Sunday lunch. You can do anything on paper. Not all of them could make it. I set up outside the atelier, among rough-cut blocks of stone: bowls, plates, cups, spoons, knives, and some anachronistic two-tined forks that caused the young butcher's wife who subsequently achieved fame as Reglindis to double up with laughter, though later she was the first of the company to spear a hot boiled potato on one. Indeed, anachronistically here too, I served potatoes with cottage cheese. They took to them all right, the alien root vegetables. Only the daughter of a Naumburg goldsmith, who posed for the master as the much later to be celebrated Uta, seemed to be disgusted by every morsel. She had a way of holding in very long fingers what she didn't want to eat. By her side, the blacksmith who resembled the lanky limestone Margrave Ekkehard, tried vainly to get the young thing to tuck in: "Go on, girl. They're not bad, these patoes or whatever they are or just call them earth apples?" Nor did she eat much of the bratwursts of which I claimed they were genuine Thuringian; whereas the others, for instance the originals for Dietmar and Timo, a couple of dyers from the outskirts who squabbled the whole time, filled their boots, so that I was fast running out of sausages on the grill. Luckily, I had laid by a couple of dozen newfangled fish sticks for an emergency; even the picky Uta found favor with those.

Quietly eating away, first with spoons, and then with knife and fork, were a cloth merchant and his wife whom the Master of Naumburg had asked to sit for him, so that Wilhelm von Camburg and his Gerburg might find some physical expression. How thoughtfully they chewed their food. To finish, there was a cold sour cherry soup with flour dumplings. Cinnamon sticks and lemon peels lent their spice. And now all, including even the future Uta with her narrow top lip and fleshy lower lip, helped themselves till the great bowl was empty. All the models, incidentally, even Gerburg, however mannerly she might be in other ways, slurped their soup.

I tried to get into conversation with the Master himself, a somewhat puny fellow one wouldn't think capable of laboring with stone. He grumbled about the variable quality of the shell limestone that was quarried in the vicinity. "Sandstone," he opined, "as extracted from the River Main would have been preferable, and not only on account of its reddish hue. Well, once it's all been cut, the gray is getting painted anyway." And then, following a pause: "I'm not really a fan of paint."—Another pause.—"Stone should be let breathe."

I wanted to know if there had been any trouble

from the Bishop, given that all the models were worldly, and without the least whiff of sacrality. He grinned impiously, and after a judicious pause, gave me to understand that the overproduction of Madonnas and saints got his goat, whether they were painted, carved in wood, or hewn in stone. "How with so much highly colored distractions, shall a man find his way to God?" The Bishop, for his part, had been happy with his human figures lending animation to the stone, with their features expressive of anger, grief, fear, but also small joys. "If they are devout and patient, then they too will be recipients of divine mercy."

I was beginning to come round to the idea that our anonymous Naumburg master might perhaps be a Waldensian, and possibly introduced some heresy from France, where he had found earlier models for his work, when he surprised me with a leap in time, anticipating Luther's Reformation and its consequences. He claimed that it was the earthly plainness of his figures that had preserved them from the fury of the iconoclasts. "They most heartily disliked that Madonna cult and the priestly proliferation of all those saints. Chopped 'em up and made kindling out of 'em!" Again, the impious grin.

And then the daughter of the goldsmith followed suit, and she too leapt ahead into the present day. The future Uta from Naumburg yelled: "Can I get a Coke?" And I was pleased that I was able to gratify the strange girl with an ice-cold Coca-Cola. Then she said: "Gorra go. Work to do. Living statue outside the cathedral gates." She was on her way, and I brought matters to a close.

Shortly after the fall of the Wall and the end of the separation it had enjoined, whereupon everything promised or threatened to be completely different, I happened to see her again—that is, in case you think chance can be trusted as an agent. I saw her not in Naumburg, the little town which you could now visit quite painlessly, without permission or supervision, but this time outside the main portals of Cologne Cathedral: or rather, methought it was her: the girl with the narrow top lip and fleshy lower lip who had once sat for the Naumburg Master.

I had an appointment with the West German radio, WDR, just by the cathedral, stepped out of the main station, and as I usually did on the short walk to the studios, took the opportunity to cast an eye on the summerly goings on below the twin towers; each time I had the sense of being at a fairground, that's how jolly and festive things are there. And there she stood, quite alone.

Now, there had for some time been a vogue for

these living statues outside our public buildings; they seemed to give expression to a prevailing mood of uncertainty, whether it be some personal sense of doom or a scientifically grounded conviction that the world was about to end. Young persons dressed as saints or mendicant friars, heretics and inquisitors, would stand for hours without moving in front of or beside the entrances to churches. Occasionally they would also perform halting, anxious gestures of benediction, before freezing again.

She, though, Uta von Naumburg, was standing directly in front of, though at some distance from the chief portal of Cologne Cathedral, so that everyone who wanted to go inside, as worshipper or visitor, had to pass on one side of her or the other. From the little crown on her head to the tips of her shoes, she was entirely gray. Her face too, and her left hand gripping her cloak were either powdered in gray or had been evenly sprayed with gray color. For her pedestal, she was standing on a little box, also gray and resembling stone. If I'd had a photograph to hand, I would have been able to compare her point by point: like her original, she wore a ring on her left index finger, bewilderingly similar to the stone ornament. The folds of her floor length cloak fell plainly without any of the stylization of Gothic. It was only where her left hand clasped the material that the pleats were interrupted. Then below the ringed hand, the cloth tumbled downward again. And just as in the widely circulated photographs, she held the collar of her cloak upright in her right hand, so that her right cheek to the point of her chin and the corresponding part of her throat and the head covering as it disappeared under the crown all remained obscured from sight. I am sure there was no bit of crenellation missing on her tiara.

And then the expression on her face. Over the curved edge of her collar, she leveled a gray-eyed and stone-faced expression upon everything in her way. What she saw seemed to be alarming, if not downright horrifying to her. Nothing could break the fixity of that look, neither the snap-happy tourists from all over the world, nor the young folk on their skates and blades, cutting shapes at a respectful distance but wildly enough. A group of Japanese visitors bowed to the stone effigy, to get their pictures taken with her.

But no one got too close to her. She kept them all at bay. Even her little gray tin alms dish waited at some distance from her. I stood by as coins kept jingling down into it, but paper money too: Deutschmarks and Dutch gulden, and a five-dollar bill. It was clear she did this professionally. And it looked as though she made a living by it as well. In all the time I watched her, she didn't allow herself a single lapse. I overcame my reluctance, and dropped a two-mark piece in her bowl, then stepped closer, still closer, then right up to her, and whispered to her, to remind her of our luncheon party: "Hallo, Uta. I was your host, remember. Why don't you take a break and get yourself an ice-cold Coke from the drinks stand over there ..."

Not a muscle. Not even a forthright: "Beat it, you old geezer!" in my direction. Or "Get lost, schmuck!" Her eyes remained fixed on whatever the approaching horror might be. Not even a twitch of the little finger on the hand clasping the collar was vouchsafed me. Eventually, a scrawny-looking fellow, no longer young, stepped up to me, and in a foreign inflected accent said: "Vould you mind keebing your distance."

Who was he? Her manager, evidently. A sort of pimp, who probably helped himself to the takings in her tin dish. Certainly no Margrave Ekkehard he, though he seemed to radiate a certain propensity for violence as well.

"It's all right, I'm going," I said, not least because I was late for my recording. I didn't even turn around to look. When I came out afterwards, she was gone. But off to one side of the continuing stream of visitors, someone had turned out in a gray hoodie, purporting to be a medieval monk, for which he received scant tribute in a cardboard box. I took the next train to Hamburg, and during the ride, jotted down sentences as though Uta had indeed spoken to me: "The Thuringian accent clearly audible. Or was the coloring more Anhaltine? But she's no Saxon, that's for sure …"

It wasn't until the following spring, after failing to see her outside the Marienkirche, either in Lübeck or in Munich, or at the cathedrals of Speyer or Worms, that I next saw Uta, stone-colored and with gray-eyed expression over the raised collar of her cloak. She stood, as though this were her regular pitch, among the cooing crowds and pigeons in front of the façade of Milan Cathedral.

I should not have taken the sculptural comment of the Naumburg Master for a mere practical tip. Outside his atelier, and in the presence of blocks of stone some still unhewn, others beginning to take shape, after our lunch, having slurped down the last of the cherry soup, and just before the girl who to him was Uta, headed off, as she mumbled, to "work" and "statue duty," he said he had in his quest for a model sought a calmly rounded, firm, and in its beauty expressionless face, of the kind that, once sculpted, would go on provoking fresh interpretations. Since the dismissive gesture he had called for provided enough in the way of expression, the viewer's eye could rest on everything and nothing. "The onlooker does most of the work anyway. He will fill up the void. I can hear it already, so much nonsense they talk."

He said it still in the presence of his model. But the goldsmith's daughter wasn't moved to put down her Coke bottle. Her mind was elsewhere.

In the present time, as I know now. The terrors of the thirteenth century were nothing to her. Compared to contemporary barbarism, either the alarms of the past had receded, or they were mingled with the current debacle, which allowed her to appear so ubiquitously as the stone original to all the visitors of Naumburg Cathedral.

"Timeless," had been the word from the cicerone of our little group in the west choir. "As an artistic product of her period, it is Uta von Naumburg who is especially dear to our hearts. It's as though she belonged to our era, as though she had emancipated herself from the prison of her class, as though she had—as we do, less distinctly—an end in view."

With this quote from the songbook of the socialist youth organization FDJ, our little group was reminded that, unlike the Staufers' former empire, the workers' and peasants' state was still extant, albeit in a lamentably crumbling condition. And two and a half years later, our wise guide, by now addressing herself to predominantly western clad visitors to her western choir, may no longer have been able to read any objective in the clear-sighted Uta; what might she see now, looming distantly or advancing ever nearer? Or perhaps her look is merely empty, and purely concerned with her own life? Then the Naumburg Master's gamble will have come off, because an empty look will always want to be filled with significance, as people set themselves to find something or nothing for it to look at.

As do I. When I saw her standing in front of the elaborate and playful façade of Milan Cathedral, she looked northern and strange in the brilliant southern light, and I was moved to ask: What is it she sees, discerns, is shocked by? Is she looking back on the last of the Staufers—Konradin to horse!—or is she haunted by the contrast between the lardy, overfed pigeons on the cathedral plaza and the millions of starving children in drought-stricken Africa? Or is she contemplating the ever-new waves of tourists always in the same gaudy apparel? And what is she doing in Milan, and not where I thought I'd find her, outside the Cathedral in Ulm?

There were other figures beside her. The usual mendicants. A Veronica with her cloth. And right next to them, but without an eye for Uta, completely gilded over, an Egyptian deity, the one with the bird on his head. Unlike her, who despite the noonday heat, didn't break sweat—at any rate, as I drew near to her as part of a Flemish tour group, I saw no glittering droplets beading on her gray skin—the godhead, dressed only in a loincloth, seemed to be melting … Under his wash of gold, he looked like … And there in the sweat-bathed Horus I thought I could make out the slightly hobbling figure of my Uta's manager, her violent pimp. I was sorely tempted to speak to him, and was already standing before his little golden bowl, but as though to punish him, didn't drop him a coin. It's him, I thought. Or at least it could be him.

But when a little later I took refuge in the shady arcade to the side of the piazza, I saw him again, dressed this time in a shirt and pants, sitting at the little table of a sidewalk café. His coffee cup was empty, his glass of water half-empty. He was reading a newspaper, as I walked past him, I thought possibly a Turkish one. Then, when I moved around behind him, seemingly looking for a place to sit, I thought I made out Arab lettering in the headlines of the opened double page. Over the top of the newspaper—of this I am sure—he could keep an eye on his living statue. He will be an Egyptian, an Algerian, no, Lebanese. He has her under his thumb. My suspicion grew blindly.

I sat four tables away from him. When he paid and left, he took his newspaper with him. I stayed behind anyway, and watched him purposefully make straight for the living statue, saw her snap out of her stony pose, saw her traipse after him step by step, weighed down with the gray box that had served as her pedestal. I am as certain as I am of anything: the bowl with the day's takings—coins and paper—had gone into his possession. The two of them disappeared in the horde of tourists. Some pigeons fluttered up. I paid. I was in a rush. Didn't want to miss my flight to Palermo. The theme of the conference I'd been invited to was literature and history. Not for the first time.

While the assembled historians and literati at the resort of Mondello worked to overcome their boredom by subtly nettling one another—the preferred charge was falsification or distortion—I continued to see before me Uta's manager and pimp, exploiting her, demanding sex from her, beating her with a leather whip because the stone gray bowl came back with too little in it; and at the same time I tried to summon up the historical Ekkehard, who props himself on his sword, behaves like a warrior anywhere outside the bed chamber, so that his wife Uta is driven to protect herself from him, with the result that the marriage remained childless and the margrave's family died out. So painfully was I preoccupied with the twofold misery of my Uta that I waded into the dispute between the writers and the historians: "We know nothing of the compulsions of the Middle Ages! The Emperor was far away, here in Palermo, completely unconcerned with what was going on at home. For instance the case of poor Uta von Naumburg, who was sexually exploited by her husband the brutal Margrave Ekkehard." Then, because my intervention had provoked only a puzzled silence, I went into detail on the donor figures in the west choir of Naumburg cathedral. When the stone Uta and her villainous margrave morphed into the present-day living statue outside Milan Cathedral (and in my rhetorical onslaught I was using rather impolite language of her limping impresario and brutal manager), the assembled historians tried to interdict this and other such leaps in time. A German Medievalist went so far as to accuse me of latent Fascism: "The Nazis constructed a racist cult around that awful Uta von Naumburg. And now you're coming to us with your completely ahistorical speculations!" Applause, bedlam. Only one Italian novelist who had set his successfully filmed novel in the so-called Dark Ages, defended my accelerated to-ing and fro-ing, pointing to the current political situation in the North and South of Italy, saying how positively medieval conditions were here and there. "Or we can cast a longer view across the Adriatic to the Balkan states, and see to our horror how murderously the Middle Ages have caught up to us."

The bickering between the professions broke out again. I kept my counsel. It was an easy matter for me to cut the next few presentations and hairsplitting debates. After a desultory inspection of historical sites going back to the times of the Staufers and Normans in Monreale and the city center of Palermo, I left the conference early, not taking a direct flight home, but stopping off in Milan. In front of the cathedral, though, there was only the usual tourist scene. My inquiries regarding one particular living statue were met with shrugs. I missed her painfully.

My pain continued. Even though work led me elsewhere, and early signs of old age suggested not only that I lead a more healthy life, but also keep firm control of my feelings, my pining didn't stop. It was as though I'd lost a lover, as though I'd been deserted, as though I had to bury something that had never been mine, but that I still needed to keep secret. I couldn't talk about it with anyone. I didn't even confess to my wife. What could I have said, in any case? A relationship, sustained over many years, to a young woman, who, for professional reasons, presented as a stone, looked through me when I stared at her, and even if I had mustered the courage to attempt a seduction, addressed her, flirted with her, would never have gone with me, because she had fallen for someone else, whom I permitted myself to hate, though only in my grimmest moods? No, there wasn't even any dalliance between us. So my wife discovered nothing, though she sensed that our little side trip to Naumburg, back when the Wall was still standing, had had consequences.

And so the years passed. And with them the century. A new currency made its appearance. And when, on my travels, I would see the still ubiquitous living statues and think of her, then I would have to imagine that she now heard the jingle of Euros in her stone-gray dish.

I didn't have much more to go on. Even my practice, gladly or in extremity to offer hospitality to my guests on paper, didn't appeal. I repeatedly invited the Anonymous Master of Naumburg and the models who represented his named donor figures to fish soup, roast saddle of venison, cheese and walnuts, but they didn't deign to come. Neither Reglindis nor Gerburg, neither Timo nor Sizzo. They remained caught in their time, or they were reluctant to be confused by the accelerated crises of our present. Our alarm about the changing weather, the threatened collapse of our state pension system, the adverse effects of globalization were all subjects they were not keen to pursue. Even Uta, whom I hoped to lure with a drinking straw and a bottle of Coca-Cola on the side didn't take up my invitation.

Auf Oldbürer Strassen
gesehen – und
im Museo Thyssen
bezeichnet mir Cranachs
Dame mit Hut und das
Fraümli woirte einer un-
bekannt Meister. (Amsterdam Hof)

I sat at table repeatedly with other guests, allowed myself to be distracted into ever remoter periods, hunkered over an open fire with guests from Neandertal, or tried my hand at Bengali cuisine; there was no shortage of distractions on offer.

When I saw her, then, no, recognized her in spite of her clothes now falling differently and her humble demeanor, she was standing, powdered in reddish rock dust, as a miracle-working saint. I ran into her, totally unexpectedly, during the Frankfurt Book Fair, when after a meal with my publishers, I found myself in the banking district. Feeling restless and homesick, I had taken off before dessert under the pretext of getting a particular brand of pipe tobacco, and there I saw her, in a part of town where tobacconists were not exactly thick on the ground.

She was in front of the Deutsche Bank. More precisely, she was standing between the main entrance and a sculpture that represented the endless circulation of money, and whose smooth abstract shape corresponded to the mirroring facades of the clumped skyscrapers. Exotic here, and yet well-placed, she stood as a Saint Elisabeth on a pedestal, which, like herself, appeared to have been hewn from red Main sandstone. Matching the little dish into which bank employees with no time to linger, no doubt also rich clients of the bank, tossed their small change. From time to time, someone from the executive floor would drop a bill. Since the place wasn't on any tourist routes, no one took selfies.

The living statue who was the spitting image of my Uta—no, she was Uta!—was holding a woven basket that also appeared to be made of stone, but lying in it were a heap of real roses, red ones, of course. They were there to illustrate the so-called rose miracle that is the subject of the legend: because Elisabeth, wife of the hard-hearted Landgrave of Thuringia, against the wishes of her lord, went out every day with a basket of bread to feed the poor, the orphans, the destitute. Her Landgrave forbade this feeding. When she persisted, and snuck out through a back door with bits and pieces of leftover crusts and crumbs—the

Landgrave ambushed her, and full of rage tore away the cloth over her basket. And lo: it was filled with budding, blooming and faded roses. The Landgrave was abashed, and changed his ways. Thenceforth, his wife had permission to take as much bread to the starving as she could. All this was several hundred years ago. And this now was the role my Uta had slipped into, although she was no canonized saint.

Her expression betrayed her. No Elisabeth could look as unerringly into blankness. And then the mouth with its narrow upper lip and thick lower lip was unmistakable. On closer inspection, the little finger on her left hand holding the basket of roses matched in its over-length the little finger that once, with the beringed index finger clumped the heavy material of her cloak into a knot of pleats. The Elisabeth outside the Deutsche Bank wore no rings as she carried her basket. And with the right, which once had raised the collar of her cloak in front of her right cheek against her husband and the rest of the world, she now doled out roses from her supply to the most generous of the bank's customers, bending gently at the hip as she did so, standing on her box.

I watched for a long time. The comings and goings at the bank. There was a steady stream of black limousines. Chauffeurs opening car doors. A few of these so-called masters of the universe took brief notice of Elisabeth and hastened on their way. A double row of police was responsible for securing the building. But the Lebanese pimp was nowhere in sight. Maybe he didn't exist anymore. He had been expatriated back to Damascus or Beirut and was taking care of business there. No longer belonging to anyone, it was possible that my Uta, now Elisabeth, was freed of inner and outer compulsions. No longer threatened with beatings and punishments and humiliations, she was able to pick and choose her parts according to her own whims and desires; today hand out rosebuds as Elisabeth of Hungary, tomorrow as Herzeleide reflect on her son Parzifal wandering about in the world. Or I could picture her as the angel with the speech bubble outside Freiburg Cathedral, or even laughing and dimpled like the jolly Reglindis, her opposite number in the west choir in Naumburg. A lot of characters suggested themselves as images. At long last, my Uta had slipped all bonds.

I was happy to see her in a warmer shade of stone, in a pleasant role, and sober import. Even the Deutsche Bank seemed bathed in a warmer light. Finally, I dared. I slipped closer, ever closer. Not that I addressed Uta, now Elisabeth, directly with a "Hello," and "Nice to see you again." Rather, in my best handwriting on a scrap of paper, I suggested that at the end of business hours at the bank, we might have a bite to eat together, and talk.

I did not give my name. Identified myself as an admirer. I didn't leave my note with the coins, but pushed it in among her remaining roses; that was how close I got to her. Uta, now Elisabeth, was just as impassive as before. That is, at least she didn't pull my missive out from the flowers, didn't feel moved to crumple it up and toss it in the direction of the sculpture that was dramatizing the continuous circulation of money. When I walked off, bowing as I went to my beloved living statue, I thought I might have caught her eye. I thought there was perhaps even a ghost of a smile.

It wasn't the tony Frankfurter Hof, the hotel beloved of Book Fair habitués that I nominated on my invitation, rather, unhesitatingly, as though following a long-prepared plan, I suggested the restaurant in the waiting room of the main station at Frankfurt; partly, because I have always liked sitting in waiting rooms, not only to kill time, partly also because I assumed that she too, my errant one, the drifter from place to place, was familiar with such places, given how often I had looked for her in waiting rooms and on railway platforms, sensing her presence there.

Six o'clock found me sitting patiently where I could keep an eye on the revolving door. I had had the table laid for two, and asked the waiter for a vase for the roses I'd hurriedly bought. As I waited, I assembled various menus in my head from the offerings on the menu, undecided as to the main course between lamb's kidneys and the popular staple of the fair city, lentil soup. Smoked salmon and herring as possible starters. For dessert, I thought chocolate mousse. I remained patient, nursed my second beer, and wasn't surprised to see her walk up to my table at a little before seven o'clock.

"Here I am," she said, "it took ages to get the makeup off." I thought I caught the lilt of Magdeburg or Halberstedt, but this was neither Uta von Naumburg nor Elisabeth of Thuringia, rather it was a woman in her early thirties, entering her maturity, who joined me at my table. No stranger. The upper and lower lip were a match, as was the over-length of the little finger. The look in her eye, even when it was directed at me, had some quality of distance, as though she was ignoring me; and she didn't seem to notice the long-stemmed roses. In the face, expressionless, as I'd expected, I looked for and found two steep furrows over her nose. Also her incessantly speaking mouth had deep folds to either side, giving her a tough, if not embittered expression. Her hair, cut short, was parted on the left, and had been dyed a reddish color. She wore cheap clips on her ears: disappointing.

And the spate of her talk! No, she didn't talk, she babbled: bland stuff about the traffic in the city center, the price of hotel rooms, the weather. In between, when she had finished complaining about her new shoes, which pinched—they had platform soles—she thanked me for the invitation: "It's really nice of you to ask me." And then, following a pause

I hoped would go on for longer, she added: "About time too, of course."

The tone was reproachful, almost harsh. Feeling sheepish and mildly guilty, I reached for the menu. She barely listened while I reeled off my suggestions like a memorized poem, only to determine, as though there was no alternative: "What the heck, I'll have what I always have, schnitzel." When I recommended a glass of light Italian red to go with it, I wasn't surprised to hear her say: "I'll just have a Coke." And as though my wine-waiterly suggestion had offended her, she added: "You know how much I like Coke." One could say that my living statue, now in beige skirt, blouse and jacket, was behaving as though thoroughly used to me.

I still didn't dare use the "Du" pronoun with her, but I cautiously started asking her questions. First, I wanted to know where she was born. She laughed, showing me some discolored teeth. "You know where. Clue: you've heard of it. Nietzsche went to school there. Novalis was from around there. When I was a kid, the boys started calling me Uta. My real name's Jutta, if you care."

So I took to addressing her as "Miss Jutta." As she had declined a starter, I went for the simpler main course. My lentil soup was brought just after her schnitzel came. She cut her meat, and went on talking with her mouth full. Shortly before the Wall came down, she went over to the West, by way of Hungary. Together with a more extroverted school friend. I learned why this girlfriend laughed so incessantly, it was to show off her dimples. This was probably said to put me in mind of Reglindis, her opposite number in the choir. But aside from the fact that the boys at school and in the Pioneers had spotted her for an Uta early on, I got to hear nothing about Naumburg, cathedral or west choir.

I didn't ask either. Everything seemed to clarify by itself. But then I did want to hear more about her Lebanese, her protective manager and—as I assumed—special pimp. I was given short shrift: "If you mean Ali, he's my boyfriend."

While Uta, whom I now had to think of as Jutta, was busy with her schnitzel—I spooned desultorily at my lentils—my notion that Ali might be Lebanese was vigorously denied. In fact Ali's name was

Herbert, his father was a Siberian German, but his mother was Kazakh, so as a believing Muslim, he had decided to change his name to Ali. "And now he's going back to Kazakhstan. It's a long story. And when he goes, I'm going with him."

When I discreetly drew her attention to the fact that I had happened in Milan to notice that her friend had been reading an Arabic newspaper, and with close attention, line by line, my observation was confirmed for me: "Oh, he knows lots of languages, not just Arabic. He picked that up as a student here in the West. I have to say, he's interested in politics. Me not so much. He can be quite fanatical. I like that about him."

Then I was informed that her boyfriend Ali had been beaten up in the course of what was presumably a political argument—he had been cursed for a Russian—and had walked with a limp ever since. "I'm talking way too much!" she exclaimed, and was through her schnitzel and her Coke. And as though by way of goodbye—"I have to go in a minute"—she had a favor to ask me. After I'd picked up the tab, she dug around in her handbag for a key for a numbered left luggage locker.

She went before I did, again with no eye for my roses. I followed with the little key, found the locker, and opened it. I took out a rather heavy package, and handed it over, no, not to Uta, but to Ali's girlfriend Jutta in the station concourse. I asked no questions and got no answers. "Till next time!" she called, and disappeared into the crowd with her parcel. That had consequences. But there was no next time.

In an era in which all over the world bombs are going off, some timed to the second, others amateurishly improvised, it could have gone unnoticed in the news, especially as damage from it was only limited; but because the place of the explosion was a neuralgic site of weal and woe, or to put it more technically, profit and loss, the attack on the Frankfurt Stock Exchange was given considerable prominence. In the grip of a deep depression following various spasms of panic, when the index seemed to have stabilized at a low level, and the experts were just beginning to see, or hope for, a glimmer on the horizon, it happened.

Outside the entrance, so to speak in the shade of the emblematic bull and bear, the device caused considerable damage. Six brokers—among them two lawyers for a society protecting the interests of small investors—were injured by flying glass and had to be taken to a nearby hospital. The animal sculptures, the bear in particular, were damaged by shards of metal. Altogether graver were the immediate financial losses that carried on well into the medium term; in memory of a long-ago crash, reference was made to another "Black Monday."

Of course, the familiar names of long-sought-after individuals and organizations came up in the headlines. A police operation got underway. There was an ongoing flight of capital. The Frankfurt Exchange, though only symbolically damaged, was urged to relocate. And only at the margins of the overexcited reporting were there some comments that referred to a lucky escape, because barely half an hour before the explosion, eyewitnesses had reported seeing a young woman standing at the entrance to the stock exchange, dressed in the garb of a medieval saint. Others had seen her there the previous week. Others again claimed that they had seen the woman back in October, identically or very similarly dressed, outside the Deutsche Bank, where she had been handing out roses to charitable brokers and other passersby. The police confirmed that she had an official permit to stand outside both bank and stock exchange.

Only when the police for a week or more had failed to come up with anything, did the saint herself, identified now as Elisabeth of Thuringia, come under suspicion. Photographs of the disguised woman appeared in the media. In spite of determined police efforts, no arrests were made. Late, again, far too late, the officials received a tip that any earlier might have been useful to them. A youth with a dog, who sold homeless publications outside inner-city sites, including also the stock exchange, had been telling everyone who would listen that he had seen the "funny saint" on the way to her pitch, but not on her way back. And where was the box she used to stand on? "Stands to reason, don't it? The bomb was hidden in the box." But who listens to a homeless man?

This all happened on 11 November, a gray, gloomy sort of day. Shortly before darkness finally fell. Although there was barely a sprinkle, it was said heavy rain had driven the saint away. In her haste, her pedestal, the suspicious box, had been forgotten. But this line of inquiry was not pursued. Before long, attention had turned to internationally sought string pullers. Conjecture as to individual suspects and the suspicious organizations behind them kept returning to the Middle East, and especially and persistently to Lebanon. I knew better.

I wouldn't have minded learning the story of Ali, of mixed German and Kazakh extraction, and his family, when I was with Uta, who when not on duty went by Jutta, eating lentils in the station restaurant, while she chomped through her schnitzel. But my living statue in civilian garb didn't like to talk about him too much. So I imagined his grandfather on his father's side was a regular Volga German. First deported to Siberia, then, following the death of Stalin the family—Mennonite farmers—resettled in Kazakhstan. There, Ali's father married or otherwise met a Kazakh woman. But when Ali, who at the time still went by Herbert, was cursed by the Kazakhs for a German, many Germans, among them Ali's father with his son, returned to Germany, where they were cursed for Russians. At that point. Ali will have remembered his Muslim mother. She had stayed behind in Kazakhstan, where she had family. Because

Ali didn't like to be cursed for a German or a Russian, he learned Arabic, and became politically engaged.

Thus or similarly the story might have gone of the lover of my living statue, told to me after she had finished her schnitzel. But all she said was that his intention was to go back to the Kazakh steppe as soon as he could, and that she was following him, come what may.

Where can she be now? Sometimes I picture her like this: standing perfectly still, wrapped in a horse blanket, somewhere in endless space. Her eye is fixed on nothing at all.

I have never gone back to Naumburg. Maybe I'll go there again sometime, with my wife, as before. We will walk through the gate in the West Lettner of the cathedral, stand in the choir, see the donor figures of Gerburg and Reglindis, Dietmar and Wilhelm von Camburg, Timo and Sizzo, Frau Gepa, the Margrave propped on his sword, and at his side his wife, who still over the raised collar of her cloak seems to see all kinds of current threats, past horrors and appalling futures.

And maybe then I will tell my wife everything, or almost everything, that I experienced with Uta, and what befell me when I was caught in the field of vision of a living statue.

Ulvshale, August 13, 2003